GW01099527

© 1997 Geddes & Grosset Ltd
Published by Geddes & Grosset Ltd,
New Lanark, Scotland.

ISBN 1 85534 815 2

Produced by Simon Girling & Associates,
Hadleigh, Suffolk.

Printed and bound in China.

10 9 8 7 6 5 4 3 2 1

SUSIE & SAM

A Day at the
Farm

GEDDES & GROSSET

It was a sunny day. Susie and Sam got up early. They were going to visit Mum's friends, Uncle Eric and Auntie Doris, who lived on a farm.

"Put on your old clothes, please," said Mum. "Farms can be messy places!"

Susie and Sam had their breakfast while Mum got their things ready.

Sam saw Mum putting his wellington boots into a bag.

"We won't need our wellies," he said. "It's not raining!"

"You'll need them all the same!" said Mum. "Now hurry up—it's time to go!"

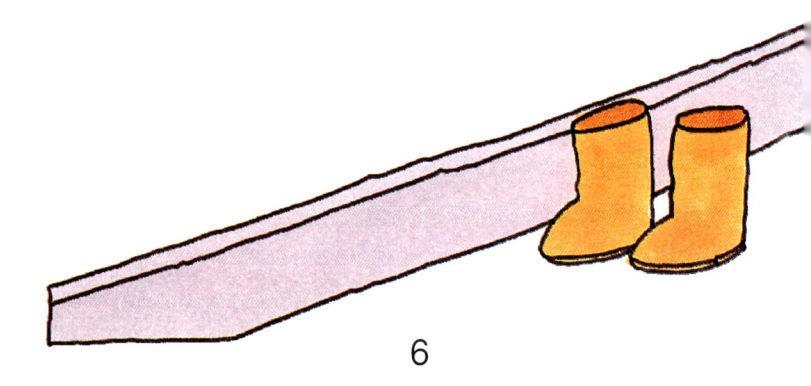

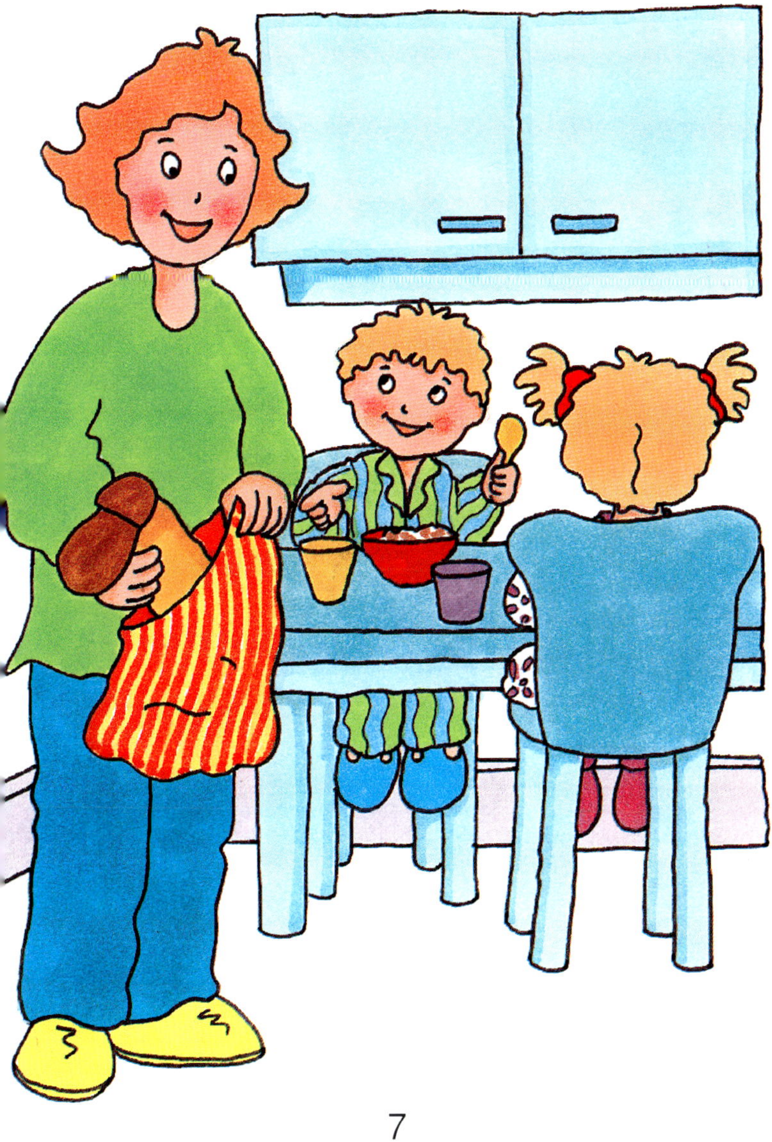

They drove away from the busy town roads into the countryside. After a while, they turned on to a bumpy track. On each side were fields with cows in them.

"These are all Eric's cows," said Mum.

"Does he have any sheep?" asked Susie.

"No," said Mum. "Eric's farm is a dairy farm. He keeps cows and sells their milk to a big dairy. Some of the milk is sold in the shops and some of it is made into cheese, butter and yoghurt."

"I didn't know that all those things were made from milk," said Susie.

Auntie Doris came out to meet them. "How lovely to see you," she said. "Uncle Eric is in the cow shed, with the vet. Some of the cows are having injections today. Would you like to go and watch?"

"Yes, please!" said Susie and Sam.

Doris showed them where to go. When they got there, the vet was just about to give the last cow her injection.

"Does it hurt the cow?" asked Sam.
"Not really," said the vet. "The cows hardly notice it at all."

He gave the cow the injection. The cow did not seem to mind it one bit.

"Are these cows ill?" asked Susie.

"No, Susie, they are not ill," said Uncle Eric. "These injections are to stop the cows from getting certain diseases."

"Can we help you to take the cows back to the field?" asked Sam.

"Yes," said Eric, "but stay by me. We don't want the cows standing on your toes!"

They said goodbye to the vet. Then Uncle Eric put two fingers in his mouth and gave a whistle. A black and white dog came running into the cow shed, wagging her tail.

"Meet Bess, my best worker," said Eric.

He opened up the pen in the cow shed. Bess went in, rounded up the cows and steered them into the farmyard.

"She's just like a sheepdog!" said Sam.

"She does a good job," said Uncle Eric. "She keeps the cows together when they are moving from one place to another."

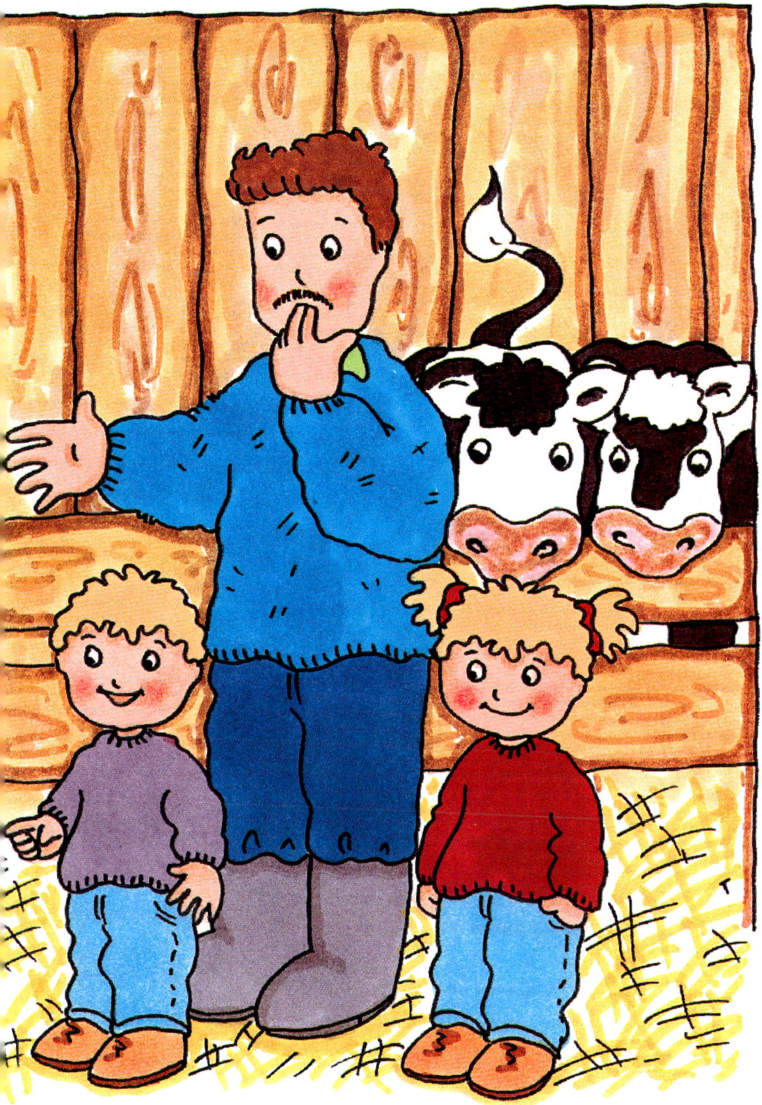

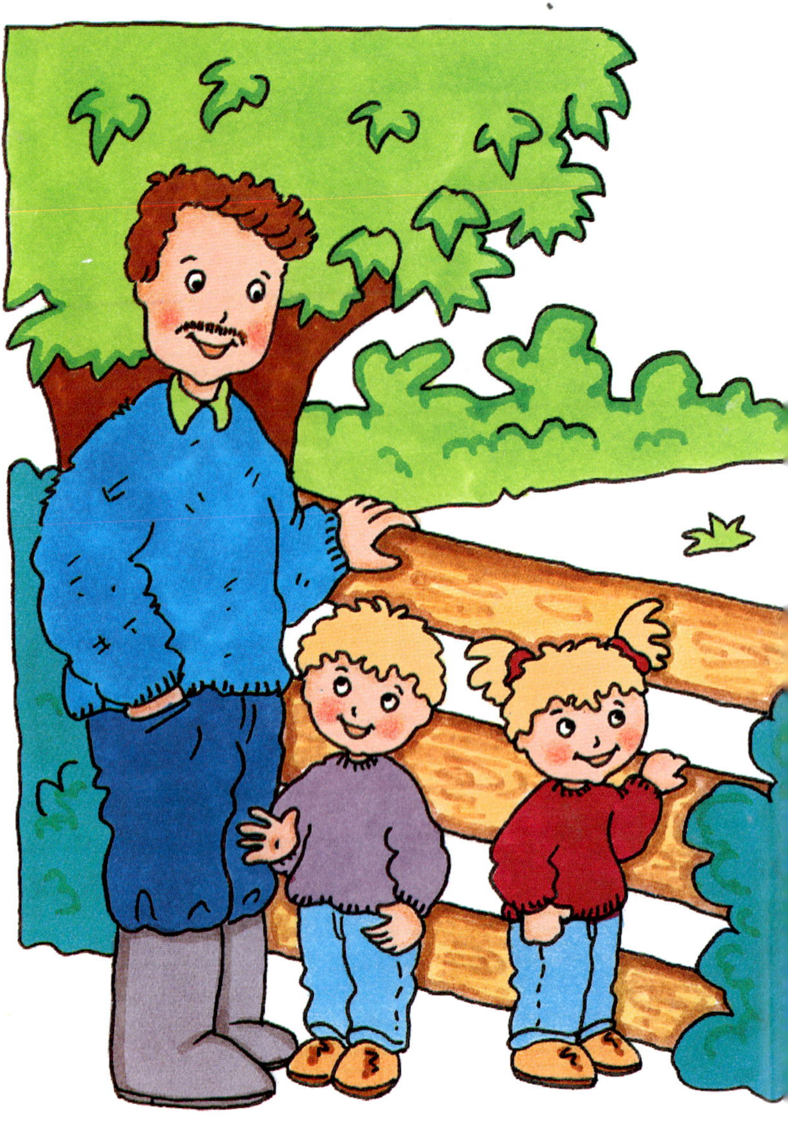

Soon the cows were back in the field.
"Do you have a bull?" asked Sam.
"Yes," said Uncle Eric.
"Is he fierce?" asked Sam.
"Not usually," said Uncle Eric. "Just so long as you don't make him cross!"

Uncle Eric took them to meet William, the bull. He had a little field all to himself. He came over to the fence to see them.

"He's big, isn't he!" said Susie.

"I'm glad he's not cross now!" said Sam.

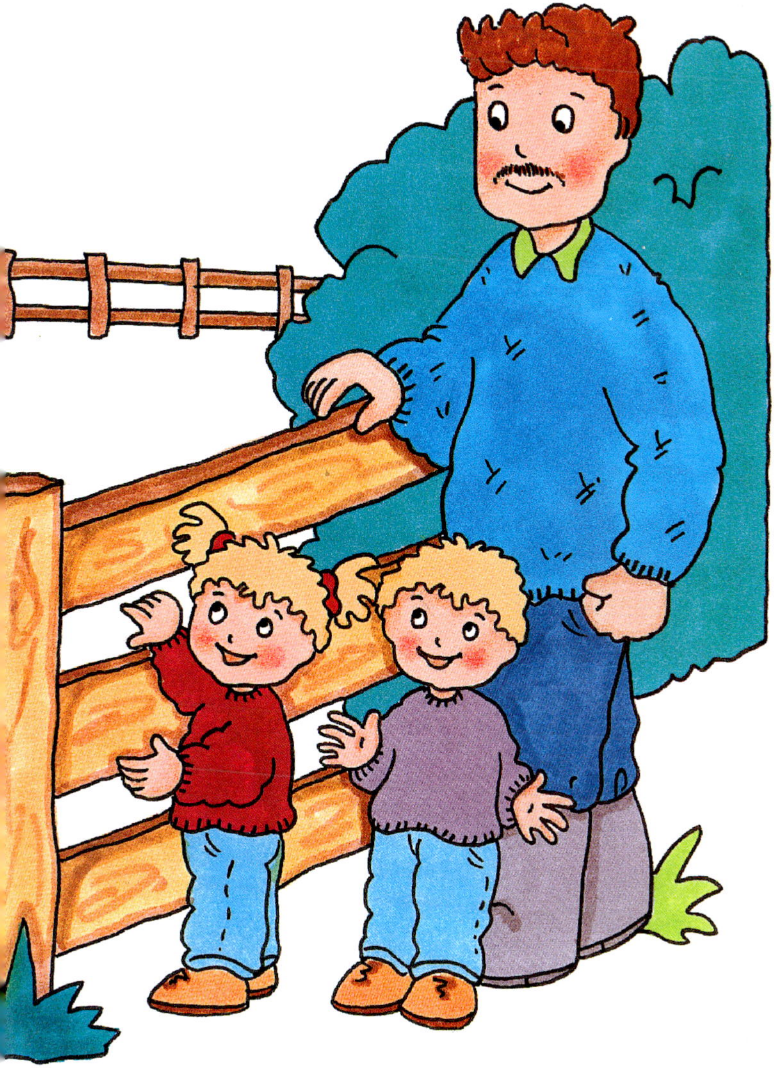

They went back to the farmhouse. Mum and Doris were making lunch.

Doris gave some carrots to Susie and Sam.

"Let's give these to Gus and Gloria," she said.

Gus and Gloria were Auntie Doris's goats. They loved the carrots.

"Watch out for Gus," said Auntie Doris. "He'll eat anything! Look, Sam, he's trying to get a tissue out of your pocket!"

Sam jumped out of the way quickly. Gus looked very disappointed.

After lunch Susie and Sam played in the farmyard.

"Stay away from the tractor," warned Uncle Eric. "Farm machinery can be very dangerous."

At milking time, Uncle Eric and Bess brought the cows into the milking shed.

"Can we watch?" asked Sam.

"Yes, but put on your wellies," said Eric.

The milking shed smelled very strange. It smelled of milk, disinfectant and animal smells.

"Why is the floor wet?" asked Sam.

"Because we have to wash it down twice a day," said Uncle Eric.

"Why?" asked Susie.

"You'll see!" said Uncle Eric.

25

Uncle Eric cleaned the udders of each cow and connected them up to the milking machines. Soon all the machines were humming busily.

Sam and Susie stood and watched.

Then, just beside Sam, one of the cows lifted her tail and something very messy happened, all over Sam's boots! Susie thought it was very funny.

"Lucky you had your wellies on, Sam!"

All too soon, it was time to say goodbye to Uncle Eric, Auntie Doris and Bess.

"Thank you for everything!" Susie and Sam called as they set off.

It had been a lovely day on the farm.

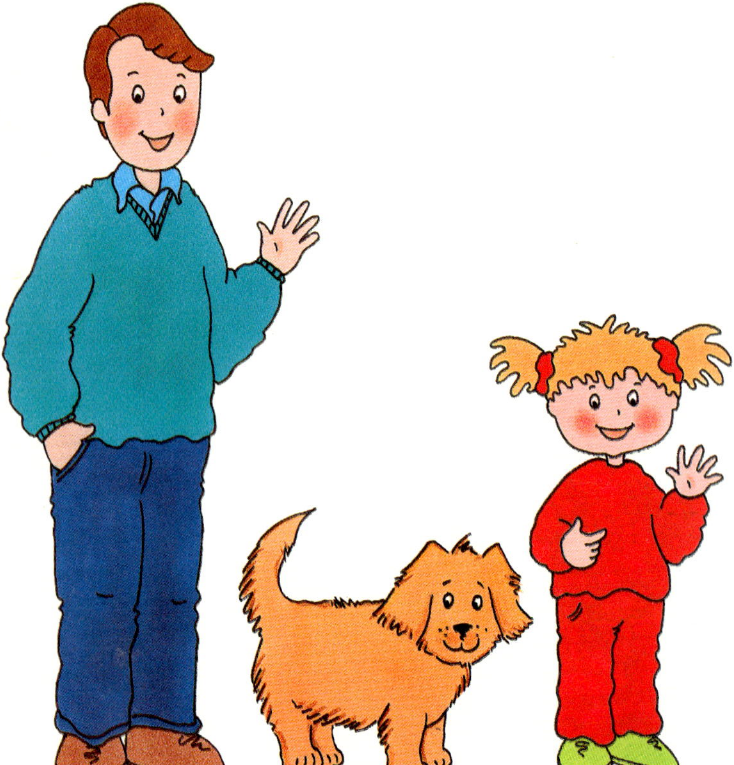